MS. Hannah Is Bananas!

MS. Hannah Is Bananas!

Dan Gutman

Pictures by Jim Paillot

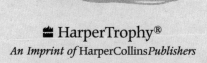

■ HarperTrophy®
An Imprint of HarperCollinsPublishers

Ms. Hannah Is Bananas!

Text copyright © 2005 by Dan Gutman

Illustrations copyright © 2005 by Jim Paillot

Library of Congress Cataloging-in-Publication Data is available.

ISBN 0-06-050706-3 (pbk.)–ISBN 0-06-050707-1 (lib. bdg.)

Typography by Nicole de las Heras

❖

First Harper Trophy edition, 2005

Visit us on the World Wide Web!

www.harperchildrens.com

17 18 19 20 OPM 50 49 48 47 46 45

To Emma

Contents

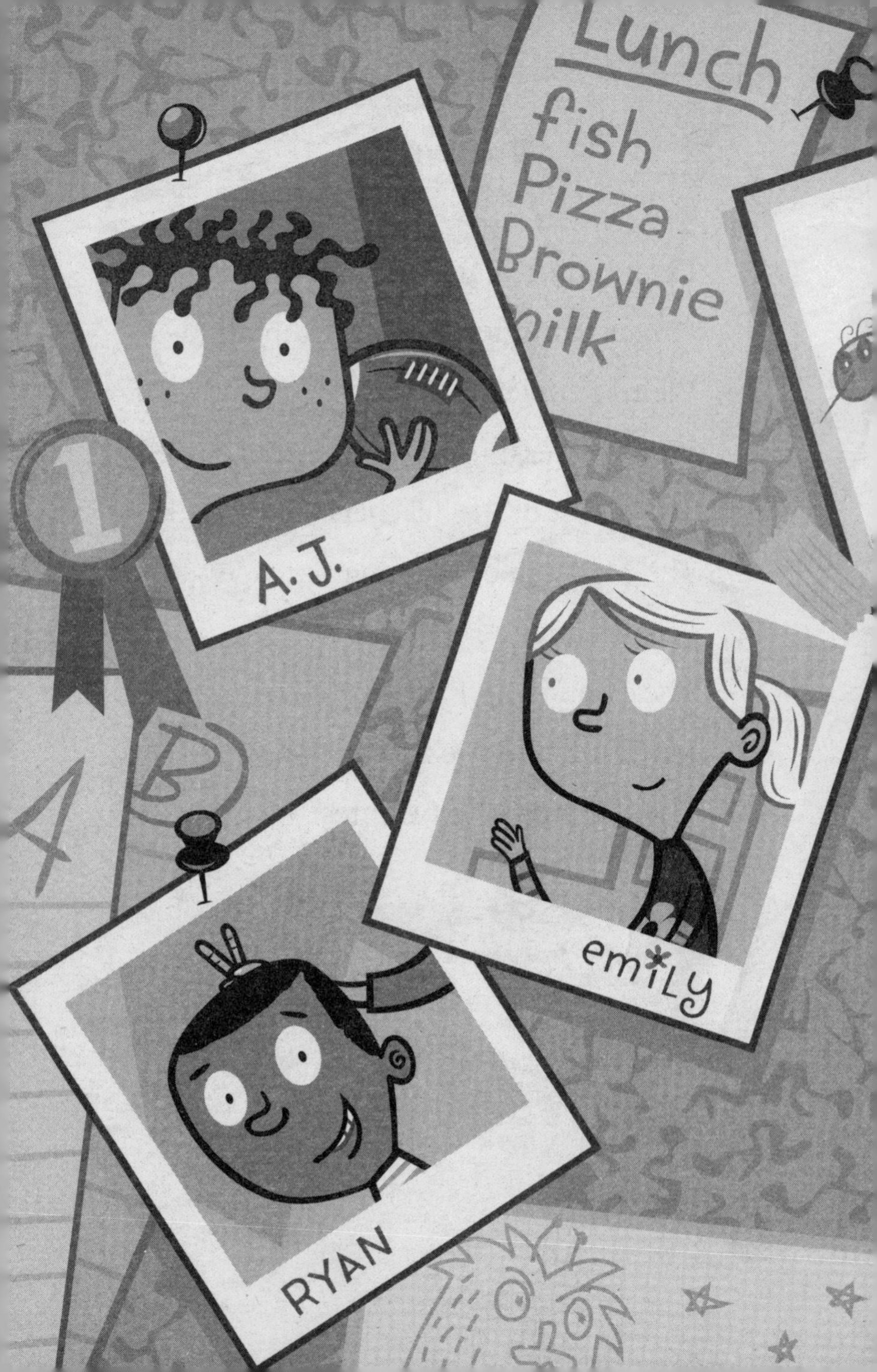
Lunch
fish
Pizza
Brownie
milk
A.J.
emily
RYAN

I Hate Andrea Young

"Miss Daisy! A.J. hit me!"

"I did not," I said.

"He did too! He bumped his elbow against my elbow!"

Andrea Young is so annoying. I barely touched her stupid elbow. She was moaning and holding her arm like an elephant stepped on it.

1

I wish an elephant would step on her *head*. Andrea has been bothering me since we were little kids. And that's a long time, because now we're in second grade.

"I saw A.J. do it, Miss Daisy," said Emily. She is Andrea's friend and is just as annoying. But in a different way.

"Am I going to have to send anyone to Mr. Klutz's office?" Miss Daisy asked.

Mr. Klutz is the principal, and that means he is like the king of the school.

"No," me and Andrea said.

"Good, because it's time for us to go to art class. I don't want you to miss it. Our art teacher, Ms. Hannah, is really nice, and I'm sure she has some fun activities planned for you."

"Art?" I said. "I hate art."

"Oh, you hate everything, A.J.," said Andrea, who thinks she knows everything.

It just so happens that I do *not* hate everything. I don't hate football. I don't hate skateboarding. I don't hate trick biking. I don't hate monster movies. Especially when the monsters crush cars and stuff. But I do hate school, and I especially hate Andrea.

"I *love* art," Andrea announced, like anybody really cared. She took out a big art box she had brought from home. It had crayons and colored pencils and other stuff in it. "When I grow up, I want to be an artist. My mom thinks I'm really creative. I like to create things."

"She should create an empty space where she is right now," I whispered to my friend Ryan, who sits in the row next to me.

"Hahahaha!" Ryan laughed, but Miss Daisy made a mean face at him and he shut up.

"Let's go, second graders!" she said. "Single file to the art room. Ms. Hannah is waiting for us."

Drawing pictures is for babies, if you ask me. And art is stupid.

Finger Painting with Ms. Hannah

Emily was the door holder. My friend Michael who never ties his shoes was the line leader. The art room was all the way on the other side of the school. We had to walk about a million hundred miles to get there. Michael told Miss Daisy it was like walking across the Grand Canyon, so she let us take drinks from the water fountain outside the art room.

That's where Ms. Hannah was standing. She was the funniest-looking lady I ever saw. She was wearing a dress that looked like it was made from a bunch of different-colored washcloths that were sewed together. On her hands were these big mittens that my mom uses when she has to take hot dishes out of the oven.

Ms. Hannah looked weird.

"Good morning, second graders," she said as we filed into the art room. "Do you like my new dress? It's made from

used pot holders that I bought on eBay. I stitched them together."

Ms. Hannah spun around so we could get the full effect of her new dress.

"It's beautiful!" Andrea said. She is always complimenting (that's a big word!) grown-ups on everything. Andrea was born old. Personally I thought it was the stupidest-looking dress in the history of the world. I went to sit with my friends Michael and Ryan, but Miss Daisy stopped us.

She told Ms. Hannah that *certain* people should not sit next to other *certain* people. I knew what that meant.

"Boy-girl-boy-girl," Miss Daisy said,

pointing to where we should sit. I had to sit at a table between Andrea and her cry-baby friend Emily.

Miss Daisy gave each of us a name tag to wear so Ms. Hannah would know our names. Then she told Ms. Hannah she would be in the teachers' lounge in case there was any trouble.

The teachers' lounge is where the teachers go when they don't have to teach.

I've never been in there. No kid has *ever* been in there in the history of the world, because kids aren't allowed inside. The teachers' lounge is like a secret club-house for teachers only.

My friend Billy from around the corner who was in second grade last year told me that they have big parties in the teachers' lounge all day long. He said the teachers dance around and play Pin the Tail on the Donkey and eat cake and take target practice with BB guns. Then they try and think up new punishments to give us kids when we misbehave.

That sounds cool. Maybe when I grow up, I'll be a teacher so I can hang out in the teachers' lounge all day and have fun.

After we sat at our tables, Ms. Hannah

took off her pot-holder mitts and picked up a piece of black paper.

"Can anyone tell me what *this* is?" she asked.

Any dumbhead knows that. I raised my hand, and she called on me. "It's a piece of black paper," I said. "Duh!"

"It *could* be a piece of black paper, A.J.," Ms. Hannah said. "But maybe it's a black cat in a coal mine. Maybe it's a crow flying in the middle of the night."

It was a trick question! I *hate* trick questions! My ears felt like they were on fire. I didn't look at anybody, but I knew everybody was looking at me and laughing to themselves.

It wasn't fair! That stupid thing was a

plain old piece of black paper, and everybody knew it.

"It looks like a piece of black paper to me," my friend Ryan said. Whew! I knew I could count on Ryan. I turned around and gave him the thumbs-up sign.

"I want you to open your imaginations, second graders," Ms. Hannah said. "Art is everything and everywhere! It's all around us! We are all artists. A dentist is an artist. Your mouth is your dentist's canvas. A man fixing a roof is an artist. You can be an artist too."

Not me, I thought to myself. Art is stupid.

Ms. Hannah put a big sheet of newspaper in front of each of us to cover the table. She took a bunch of old T-shirts out of the closet and gave one to everybody to wear so we wouldn't get paint all over ourselves. Then she put paint in the middle of all the tables and gave each of us a piece of white paper.

"Today we are going to finger paint," she said.

"I'm not painting *my* fingers," I said. Some of the kids laughed, even though I didn't say anything funny.

"You silly dumbhead," Andrea said. "Finger painting is when you use your fingers to paint pictures."

I knew that. Andrea thinks she knows everything.

"What should we paint?" Emily asked

Ms. Hannah.

"Anything you like! Express your creativity. Paint what you love."

"I love butterflies," Andrea said. "I'm going to finger paint a picture of a happy family of butterflies."

"I'm going to finger paint a picture of a tree in a forest where your butterflies can live," said Emily.

"I'm going to finger paint a picture of a tree falling in a forest and crushing a family of happy butterflies until they are dead," I said.

"That's mean!" Emily said. She looked like she was going to cry, like she does at every stupid little thing.

"Hey, I'm just expressing myself," I said.

I turned around and saw that Ryan was finger painting an airplane. Michael was finger painting a house. Everybody was hard at work finger painting.

The finger paint looked yucky to me. I didn't really want to get it all over my hands. It was disgusting. I just sat there watching everybody finger paint. My piece of paper was the only one that was perfectly white.

"Why aren't you finger painting, A.J.?" Emily whispered to me.

"Mind your own business, dumbhead."

"Ms. Hannah!" Andrea called out. "A.J. isn't finger painting."

Andrea is a big tattletale. She stuck out her tongue at me as Ms. Hannah came over to our table.

"A.J., you haven't finger painted a thing," Ms. Hannah said.

I didn't know what to do. I didn't know what to say. I had to think fast. "I did too finger paint something," I said. "This is a picture of a white polar bear. He's playing in the snow. *White* snow. And he's eating . . . vanilla ice cream!"

All the kids were looking at me. Ms. Hannah was looking at me. I was afraid she was going to yell or go get Miss Daisy from the teachers' lounge to take me to the principal's office.

"Very nice finger painting, A.J!" Ms. Hannah said with a big smile on her face. "That's using your creativity!"

Hahaha! I stuck my tongue out at Andrea. She folded her arms across her front all mad-like.

It was great. It was not only great. It was the greatest moment in the history of the world. This was the next best thing to an elephant stepping on Andrea's head.

Pretty soon it was time to clean up. Ms. Hannah taught us a song about cleaning up. The words were, "Clean up, clean up, everybody everywhere. Clean up, clean up, everybody do their share."

It was a pretty dumb song, and me and Michael and Ryan changed the words to "Clean up, clean up, even in your underwear."

Any time anybody says a word that rhymes with "air," you should always change it to "underwear." Everybody will laugh. Believe me, this works *every* time.

Ms. Hannah peeled the sheets of painty newspaper off our desks and stuck them on a ball that was sitting on the windowsill. The ball was about the size of a beach ball.

"What are you doing, Ms. Hannah?" Michael asked.

"I'm making a newspaper ball," she said.

"Why?" we all asked.

"Old newspapers with paint all over them can be art. This is my art. Like I said, art is every- where. And this way, nothing goes to waste. I don't like waste. If you look around,

you'll see that I don't even have a garbage can in here."

We looked around. It was true. There was no garbage can in the art room. Ms. Hannah didn't need a garbage can, because she never threw anything away. "That reminds me," Ms. Hannah said. "For our next class, I would like you all to bring in things from home that your parents were planning to throw away."

"What for?"

"So we can make them into art."

I was still looking around for a garbage can. She had to have a garbage can *somewhere*. Everybody needs a garbage can.

"It's a shame when people throw things

away," Ms. Hannah said. "Everything in the world is beautiful. Everything can be used to make some kind of art."

"Well, I just blew my nose," I said, holding out a tissue. "Does that make my boogers artistic?" Everybody laughed even though I didn't say anything funny. Ms. Hannah took my tissue and stuck it to her big newspaper ball.

It was disgusting.

Weird People

In the lunchroom I got to sit next to Ryan and Michael. I gave my apple to Ryan, and he gave me his yogurt with sprinkles in it.

"Ms. Hannah is weird," I said.

"Artists are always weird," Ryan said. "My mom has a friend who's an artist,

and she's really weird. My mom says
that's because artists are creative."

"Your mom is weird," Michael said.

"Lots of people are weird," I told them.
"That doesn't make them creative. Some
people are just weird, and they're not creative at all. And some people are creative,
and they're not at all weird."

"You're weird, A.J.," Ryan said.

"Anybody who wears a dress made of pot holders is weird," Michael said.

"Art teachers are supposed to dress funny," I said.

"If my dad dressed like that, he'd be fired," Ryan said.

"Your dad is a businessman," Michael told Ryan. "He has to wear a tie around his neck every day. It doesn't do anything. It's just a piece of cloth that hangs around his neck. If you ask me, that's pretty weird."

"Yeah," I said, "which is weirder, wearing a dress made out of pot holders, or wearing a piece of cloth around your neck for no reason at all?"

"They're both weird," Ryan said.

"All grown-ups are weird, especially art teachers," said Michael.

"Ms. Hannah is weird, even for an art teacher," I said. I noticed that Andrea and Emily at the next table were listening to us. I knew they were listening because they kept shaking their heads and rolling their eyes and snickering at us.

"Maybe Ms. Hannah isn't really an art teacher at all," I said, just loud enough so the girls would hear it. "Did you ever think about that? Maybe she's just pretending to be an art teacher."

"Yeah!" Michael said. "Maybe Ms. Hannah is a thief, and she's trying to steal all our garbage and take over the world. Stuff like that happens in comic books all the time."

"Maybe our real art teacher was kidnapped, and she's tied up to a chair in the teachers' lounge," Ryan said.

"And the teachers are shooting BB guns at her," I added.

"We've got to save her!" Emily suddenly said. There were tears running down her cheeks. Then she got up and went running out of the room.

Me and Ryan and Michael laughed our heads off. That Emily is such a crybaby.

"You boys are weird," Andrea said.

What a Mess!

The next time we had art class, the newspaper ball that Ms. Hannah had been making was *huge*! It was about as high as a desk. Everybody wanted to touch it. Everyone except for me, that is. I remembered that somewhere inside that ball was my booger.

The art room was filled with all kinds of junk kids brought in from home. There were old musical instruments, broken toys, soda cans, plastic wrap, and all kinds of garbage. You should have seen it! Some kid brought in a tennis racquet with no strings.

"What a mess!" Emily said.

"If my bedroom looked like this, my mom would go crazy," Michael said. "You should throw half this stuff in the garbage, Ms. Hannah."

"Oh dear, no," she said. "I don't like to throw things away. In fact, at home the garbagemen bring *me* garbage so I can use it in my art. When I have a day off, I go to junkyards looking for treasures."

Ms. Hannah is bananas!

She had some sticky glue that sticks to everything. She told us to make a sculpture out of the junk kids brought in from home.

"Express yourself!" Ms. Hannah said. "Show your creativity! Remember, art is everywhere. Art is light. Art is air. Even things that are invisible can be art."

Michael started making a robot out of toilet paper tubes. Emily made a doll out of buttons.

I didn't know what to make. I think I'm just not very artistic. I didn't feel like gluing a bunch of junk together. Ms. Hannah walked around looking at everyone's sculptures and telling them how wonderful they were. I hoped Ms. Hannah wouldn't come over to me.

"A.J. isn't making a sculpture," Andrea said, and she stuck her tongue out at me. I hate her.

"Why aren't you making anything, A.J.?"

I didn't know what to do. I didn't know what to say. I had to think fast. "I did make a sculpture," I said. "This is an invisible sculpture. I call it 'The Invisible Sculpture.'"

"Very clever, A.J.!" Ms. Hannah said. "That's using your creativity!"

I stuck out my tongue at Andrea.

"I have an announcement, second

grade," Ms. Hannah said after clean-up time. "Mr. Klutz has agreed to sponsor a big art contest. There will be a prize for the winner in each grade."

"What's the prize?" Ryan asked.

"A gift certificate for a hundred dollars to an art supply store."

Everybody went "ooh" and "wow." It didn't seem like a great prize to me. I don't like art. What would I do with a bunch of art supplies?

Ms. Hannah said we had to create our artwork at home and bring it in two weeks later if we wanted to be in the contest.

"You can make anything you like," Ms. Hannah said, "and use whatever materials you want. Freely express yourselves!

Creativity is the most important thing."

"Can we just draw pictures?" Michael asked.

"Of course!" said Ms. Hannah.

"I hope I win," I heard Andrea whisper to Emily. "I'm going to make a sculpture with butterflies."

I hate her. I wonder if there are poisonous butterflies that bite people.

"So who thinks they might enter the contest?" asked Ms. Hannah. Everybody raised their hands except for me.

"What about you, A.J.?"

I didn't say anything. But I'll tell you what I was thinking: I hate art! Art is stupid!

The Secret of the Teachers' Lounge

We were out in the playground during recess. Me and Ryan and Michael all agreed that Ms. Hannah was weird. I mean, saving all that garbage is good for the environment and all, but it's kind of weird, too. She doesn't have enough garbage of her own. She has to go get *other* people's garbage.

"She's not an art teacher," I said. "She's a garbage collector."

"I still say our real art teacher was kidnapped," Ryan said. "She's probably tied up to a chair in the teachers' lounge."

The teachers' lounge is on the second floor of our school. Ryan said he thought it was in a room over the playground. We looked up at the windows and found the one that was probably the teachers' lounge.

"Our real art teacher could be in there right now," Ryan said, "tied up to a chair and being tortured!"

"Too bad we're too short to see inside," Michael said.

That's when I came up with the most genius idea in the history of the world.

I told Ryan and Michael that we might be able to see inside the window to the teachers' lounge if we stood on top of each other.

Michael got down on his hands and knees below the window. Ryan climbed up on top of him and hunched down. I climbed up on top of Ryan and stood on his shoulders.

"Can you see anything, A.J.?" Michael grunted.

"Not yet."

I could almost see into the window. I grabbed hold of the ledge on the window to pull myself up better.

"Hurry up!" Michael said. "My back is going to break!"

That's when I saw them. The teachers! I saw Miss Daisy and Mrs. Roopy and a few of the other teachers. I was looking right into the teachers' top-secret lounge!

"I see them!" I shouted.

"What are they doing?" Ryan asked, all excited.

"Not much," I said.

"Is anybody tied up to a chair?" Michael asked.

"No."

"Are they dancing around with each other?" Ryan asked.

"No."

"Are they playing Pin the Tail on the

Donkey?" Michael asked.

"No," I said. "They're just sitting there . . . eating lunch."

"That's *it*?" Ryan said.

"Wait!" I told them. "Mrs. Roopy is getting something out of the closet!"

"Is it a BB gun?" Michael asked.

"No, it's a paper bag," I said. "It must be her lunch."

"This is boring," Ryan said.

"One more minute," I said.

"My back is breaking!" Michael hollered.

I don't know exactly what happened next, but all I knew was that Ryan and Michael weren't holding me up anymore. *Nothing* was holding me up anymore.

I was holding on to the ledge of the windowsill with my elbows. If I let go, I would fall. I was afraid my head would bang on the windowsill.

"Help! Help!" I shouted.

I was hanging there for about a million hundred minutes until some of the teachers inside the teachers' lounge noticed me. They rushed over and opened the window.

"A.J., what are you doing out here?" Miss Daisy said as she and the other teachers pulled me inside.

"Uh, I was just hanging around," I told them.

The Museum of Hanging Garbage

For a few days, I was the star of the school. No kid had *ever* been inside the teachers' lounge. I was probably the first one in the history of the world.

Everybody wanted to know about the incredible things I saw in the teachers' lounge. Kids were even offering me candy to tell them.

I didn't want to tell them the teachers' lounge was just a boring old room where the teachers sat around eating lunch. I didn't want to lie, either. So I just told them that the teachers blindfolded me and said they would torture me if I ever revealed what went on in the teachers' lounge. It was cool.

Our next art class wasn't an art class at all. Ms. Hannah took us on a field trip to a museum.

I hate museums. Museums are boring.

"Why don't we ever take a field trip to a cool place like a skateboard park?" I asked Ryan on the bus ride over to the museum.

"What's so great about skateboard parks?" Andrea asked from the seat in front of me.

"Well, for one thing, *you're* not there," I said. Ryan laughed.

Andrea made a mean face at me. "I like museums," she said. "My mom takes me to museums all the time."

"Too bad she doesn't leave you there," I said.

Ryan laughed.

We walked around the museum for about a million hundred hours. Ms. Hannah was all excited. She just about ran from room to room telling us about all the wonderful art.

It was horrible and boring, and I was hungry and my legs were tired. I looked for a place to sit down.

There were some big boxes of soup cans in the corner, and I went to take a rest on them. But as soon as I sat down, all these loud bells started ringing and guards came running over. One of them was blowing a whistle, and he started yelling at me.

"Get up!" he
shouted. "You
can't sit there!"

"Okay, okay!" I said,
getting up fast. "I'll sit someplace else."
What's the big deal? I wondered.

The guard looked like he was going
to arrest me or something. Luckily Ms.
Hannah ran over and rescued me. I asked
her what I did, and she told me that I had

sat on some art.

"That's art?" I asked. "I thought it was boxes of soup."

"It's *modern* art!" she said. "That is a famous sculpture that is worth millions of dollars."

It looked like soup boxes to me. Ms. Hannah told me to remember that art is everywhere, so I should be careful what I sat on. She put her arm around me and kept it there for the rest of the time we were in the museum.

We walked around and she kept pointing out the beautiful artwork all over the place.

"Look at this!" she kept saying. "Isn't it marvelous?"

We stopped in front of a painting. It was just a bunch of lines and squares and box shapes. It was really stupid.

"Isn't it wonderful?" Ms. Hannah said. "It's called 'Broadway Boogie Woogie.'"

"My little sister could paint that with her eyes closed," I said.

The next room didn't have any paintings on the walls at all. But all kinds of junk was hanging from the ceiling.

"Can anybody tell me what these are?" Ms. Hannah asked us.

"That must be the museum's garbage," I told her. "When my family goes camping, we hang our garbage from a tree so the bears and raccoons don't get it."

"They don't have bears and raccoons

in museums, dumbhead," Andrea said. "Those things are called mobiles."

"That's right, Andrea!" Ms. Hannah said, and Andrea stuck her tongue out at me. I hate her. "They are also called kinetic sculptures."

"What does that mean?" Emily asked.

"It means it comes from Connecticut," I told her.

"No, *kinetic* means 'movement,'" Ms. Hannah said. "The sculptures can move."

"Don't tell me *that's* art," I said, looking at one of those Connecticut things.

"Not only is this art," Ms. Hannah said, "it's a masterpiece!"

"Looks like hanging garbage to me," I

said. This museum was the weirdest museum in the history of museums. I was bored and hungry, and I wanted to sit down. Finally Ms. Hannah said we could go outside in the garden and have a snack.

"Before we leave the museum," she started, "does anybody have any questions?"

I raised my hand. "If all of the stuff in here is art, how do they know what to throw away as garbage?" I asked. "Do they ever throw the art away by accident and leave the garbage here? How do they know which is which?"

Everybody laughed even though I

didn't say anything funny. I never did find out how they threw their garbage away.

Performance Art

There's a garden in the back of the Museum of Hanging Garbage. We went out there, and Ms. Hannah gave out pretzels and punch to all of us. She said we could run around and burn off some energy.

We were munching the pretzels when

Michael noticed a statue at the other end of the garden. It was a statue of a guy. He was dressed in a raincoat and he was holding an umbrella. The cool thing was that the statue guy was painted gold from head to toe.

"Now *that* is cool," I said.

A bunch of people were standing around in a circle looking at the statue guy.

"Hey, wait a minute!" Michael said. "I just saw that statue guy move."

"He did not," I said.

"Did too," said Michael.

I went over to the statue guy. There was a hat on the ground in front of him, and there was money in it. That was weird. If it was a statue, why would anybody give it money?

The statue guy wasn't moving at all. I walked around him real slow. I said "Boo!" to him. He didn't move. I wanted to touch him to see if he was a real statue, but I was scared.

I looked in the statue guy's eyes. They sure looked real, but he wasn't moving a muscle.

"See, I told you," I said to Michael. "It's just a stat—"

But just as I said it, the statue guy suddenly picked up his hand and put it on my head!

I screamed and jumped about three feet in the air! All the people who were watching started to laugh even though there wasn't anything funny about it.

I hadn't been so scared since I went to this haunted mansion on Halloween and

all these zombies were jumping out from behind the walls. When that statue guy moved, I thought I was going to die.

Ms. Hannah came over and put her arm around me.

"See, that's art too, A.J.!" she said as she put some money in the statue guy's hat. "This man has turned himself into a work of art! It's just like I always tell you. Art is everywhere. This is called perform-ance art!"

Performance art? Performance art? I think maybe when I grow up, I will paint myself gold and stand around doing nothing but scaring kids all day. That per-formance art stuff is cool.

The Friendship Picture

When we got back to school, Ms. Hannah took us to the art room. What a mess!

There was more junk than ever in there. Her newspaper ball was bigger too. It was almost as tall as me.

Ms. Hannah said she hoped the art we saw in the museum had inspired us to create art on our own. She passed out paper and pencils and said that today we were going to draw friendship pictures.

"What's a friendship picture?" Emily asked.

"A friendship picture is a picture that two people draw together," she said.

"That sounds like fun," said Andrea. "Can Emily and I work on a friendship picture together? We're best friends."

"Can I draw a picture with A.J.?" asked Ryan.

"No," said Ms. Hannah. "I want Andrea and A.J. to work on a friendship picture together."

Everybody laughed even though Ms.

Hannah didn't say anything funny. That's because everybody knows that Andrea and I hate each other.

"Do I have to work with *him*?" Andrea asked.

"Do I have to work with *her*?" I asked.

"Yes," said Ms. Hannah. "Andrea, you love butterflies, right? A.J., you love skateboards. Let's see the two of you draw a skateboarding butterfly."

We got to work. Andrea drew the butterfly and the background. I drew a helmet on the butterfly, a skateboard under it, and a bunch of ramps and stuff.

Our friendship picture actually came out pretty good. Ms. Hannah was so impressed at how well me and Andrea worked together that she went to get Miss Daisy.

"Hey, this is pretty cool," I said, holding up our friendship picture.

"Wow," agreed Andrea, taking the friendship picture. "I'm going to take this home so my mom can put it up on the refrigerator."

"I want to take it home," I said, grabbing the friendship picture away from Andrea. "My mom will want to put it up on *our* refrigerator."

"You hate art, A.J.," Andrea said, grabbing the friendship picture back. "Why should *you* get to take it home?"

"Because I want it, that's why," I said. I grabbed the friendship picture back from Andrea. Only this time Andrea didn't let go.

She pulled on one side of the friend-ship picture. I pulled on the other side of the friendship picture. That's when our

friendship picture ripped right down the middle.

"You ruined our friendship picture!" Andrea shouted.

"I did not! You did!"

"I hate you!"

"I hate you back!"

I heard Ms. Hannah and Miss Daisy coming down the hall toward the art room.

"Wait until you see how well A.J. and Andrea are working together," Ms. Hannah said as they walked into the room. "You won't believe your eyes."

9

Mr. Klutz and the Secret Drawer

"You two," Miss Daisy said. "Go to Mr. Klutz's office. Now."

"Ooooooooooooooh!"

I thought Andrea was going to kill me on the way to the principal's office. She was really mad. Andrea had never been to Mr. Klutz's office before. That's because she never does anything wrong.

"I can't believe I'm in trouble," Andrea said. "It's all your fault, A.J."

"Relax," I said. "I've been to the principal's office plenty of times. Mr. Klutz is a good guy."

Mr. Klutz was sitting at his desk talking on the phone when we arrived. He is not only the principal of the school, but he also has no hair at all.

Once he let everybody in our class touch his head. It was cool.

"Are we going to be punished?" Andrea asked when Mr. Klutz hung up the phone. She was all nervous and talked in a quiet voice.

"I don't believe in punishing children," Mr. Klutz said. "I believe in rewarding children for doing good things. Now tell me, why can't you two get along?"

"He says mean things to me," Andrea said.

"She thinks she knows everything," I said.

"He hates everything."

"Not everything. Just you."

Mr. Klutz leaned forward in his chair and rubbed his forehead. Grown-ups always rub their foreheads when they are thinking. I guess it must help their brains work better. When you get old, your brain doesn't work as good anymore so you have to rub your forehead to get it going again.

"What can we do to solve this problem?" Mr. Klutz asked.

"Kick A.J. out of school."

"Kick Andrea out of school."

"I'm not kicking *anyone* out of school," Mr. Klutz said. "The two of you are going to have to live with each other."

"In the same house?" I asked. "I thought you said you don't punish kids."

Mr. Klutz laughed even though I didn't say anything funny. Then he took a key and opened one of his desk drawers. The drawer was filled all the way up to the top with candy. Chocolates. Lollipops.

Caramels. He had like a whole candy shop in his drawer. I decided right there that I want to be a principal when I grow up.

"Would you like some of this?" Mr. Klutz asked us.

Andrea and I nodded our heads and licked our lips.

"Here's the deal. If you two can go a full day without fighting, I will give you each a candy bar tomorrow."

"How about two candy bars?" I suggested.

"One candy bar each," Mr. Klutz said. "That's my final offer. Take it or leave it."

I don't like Andrea. She doesn't like me either. But we both like candy bars.

I would have to go one day without fighting with Andrea. One day wasn't so long. I could handle one day.

"Okay," Andrea and I said.

Then we all shook on it. Shook hands, I mean. We didn't just start shaking.

That would have been dumb.

The Big Stupid Art Contest

The next morning I was on my best behavior. I was trying very hard to not say anything mean to Andrea.

But it wasn't easy, because she is so annoying. When Andrea gave an apple to Miss Daisy as a present, I wanted to say something mean. But I didn't.

When Andrea showed everybody the A+ she got on the math quiz, I wanted to say something mean. But I didn't.

When Andrea told Miss Daisy how pretty her hair looked, I wanted to say something mean. But I didn't.

Andrea wasn't saying anything mean to me either. We both wanted that candy bar.

Miss Daisy was happy that Andrea and I were being so nice to each other.

When it came time for lunch, she sat us at the same table with Ryan and Michael and Emily. I traded Emily my banana, and she traded me her potato chips.

"Did you all bring in your stuff for the

art contest?" asked Emily. "Ms. Hannah is going to judge the winner this afternoon."

I had forgotten all about the stupid art contest. Michael said he made a statue out of toothpicks. Ryan said he made a papier-mâché head. Emily made a collage. Andrea made a mobile with hanging butterflies (of course!).

I was the only one who didn't bring in anything. I hate art. Art is stupid.

"Did you see the art room?" Andrea asked. "When I brought my mobile in, the place was just a big mess."

"Of course it's a big mess," Ryan said. "Have you ever seen Ms. Hannah throw anything away?"

"She can't throw anything away," Michael said. "She doesn't have a garbage can."

"That's exactly what I mean," Andrea said. "Ms. Hannah just gets more and more stuff, and never throws anything away. My mother is a psychologist. She helps people with their problems. And my mother says that people who can't throw anything away have a problem."

I was going to tell Andrea that *she* was the one who had a problem. But I didn't. I wanted that candy bar.

"You know, everything *isn't* art," Andrea said. "Some things are garbage. Maybe Ms. Hannah became an art teacher because she couldn't throw anything away. She might be a sick, sick woman who needs help."

"I never thought of it that way," Ryan said.

"We've got to help her!" said Emily.

"What can we do?" asked Michael.

"I've got an idea!" said Emily. "Why don't we sneak into the art room during recess and clean it up? When Ms. Hannah sees how neat and clean everything is, she will realize she has a problem."

"That's a great idea!" Andrea said.

It didn't sound like such a great idea to me. Cleaning things up was no fun at all. I don't like cleaning my room at home. I sure didn't want to clean up the art room. But I didn't want to get into an argument with Andrea either. If we had a fight, I wouldn't get my candy bar.

After we finished lunch, the five of us snuck down the hall to the art room.

Andrea was right. The place was a big mess. That's when I came up with the greatest idea in the history of the world.

"You know what?" I said. "Instead of

cleaning this place, we should mess it up even worse."

"Why would you want to do that?" Emily asked.

"If we really mess it up bad, Ms. Hannah will be so shocked that she will realize she has a problem."

It sounded like a genius idea to me. Cleaning isn't fun at all, but messing things up is lots of fun.

"I'm not sure that's such a good idea, A.J.," Andrea said.

"Sure it's a good idea," I said.

"Trust me, A.J. It's not a good idea."

Andrea thinks she knows everything. Well, she doesn't know everything.

"I'm not cleaning this place up," I said. "I'd rather go outside for recess."

"You promised you would help," Andrea said.

"I did not."

"Did too."

"I hate you, A.J.!"

That's when Andrea did the dumbest thing in the history of the world. She pushed me.

If I knew she was going to do something dumb like that, I could have gotten ready for it. But how was I to know she was going to do something dumb like push me?

My foot must have slipped or

something, because I fell backward.

Right behind me was Ms. Hannah's newspaper ball. When I fell backward, I landed on top of the ball.

The ball rolled. I rolled on top of it.

"Watch out!" Emily screamed.

My foot hit Andrea's butterfly mobile that was hanging from the ceiling. The butterfly mobile landed on my head.

On the floor behind the ball were a bunch of cans of paint. I tried to get out of the way, but I couldn't. When I hit the ground, I hit the paint first.

"You stupid dumbhead!" Andrea shouted. "You crushed my butterflies!"

"You pushed me into them!"

"I did not! You fell on them on purpose!"

I got up off the floor. Paint and butterflies were all over me. Red. Yellow. Blue. Green. It was cool.

"Hey, look!" I said. "Art is everywhere." Ryan and Michael laughed.

"How can you make jokes at a time like this?" Andrea said. "You ruined my mobile! Now I won't win the contest!"

"You're going to be in big trouble, A.J.," Emily said.

"Somebody's coming," Ryan said.

"Everybody shut up!"

That's when the door opened. Ms. Hannah and Mr. Klutz came in. I was standing there with paint and Andrea's stupid butterflies hanging all over me.

"What's the meaning of this?" Mr. Klutz asked. I didn't know what to do. I didn't know what to say. I had to think fast.

"It's . . . performance art," I said.

Everybody looked at me for like a million hundred seconds.

"Yeah," Andrea finally said. "It's *friendship* performance art. A.J. and I made it together."

Ms. Hannah walked around me and looked me over. One of the butterflies slid down my head and stopped at the end of my nose.

"It's Connecticut friendship perform-ance art," I said.

"I think it's fabulous!" Ms. Hannah said. "It is so very creative. I believe the winners of the art contest are Andrea and A.J.!"

Everybody cheered and clapped. Mr. Klutz reached into his jacket pocket and pulled out two candy bars.

"I'm so pleased to see the two of you are getting along so well together," he said. "I promised you each a little something if you could go a day without fighting. Here is your prize. Congratulations!"

The candy bar tasted great. Maybe art isn't so stupid after all.

After it was all over, I still hated Andrea. Andrea still hated me. Ms. Hannah still had a big problem with collecting garbage. I said I would try to be nice to Andrea. She said she would try to be nice to me. And we both said we would try to help Ms. Hannah with her problem.

But it won't be easy!

Also in the **My Weird School** series

Pb 0-06-050700-4

#1: Miss Daisy Is Crazy!

Something weird is going on! A.J. is a second grader who hates school—and can't believe his teacher hates it too!

Pb 0-06-050702-0

#2: Mr. Klutz Is Nuts!

The second book in this wacky and hilarious series stars A.J. again—and he can't believe his crazy principal wants to climb to the top of the flagpole!

Pb 0-06-050704-7

#3: Mrs. Roopy Is Loopy!

The new librarian at A.J.'s weird school starts dressing up as different historical characters, and A.J. and his friends think she's gone completely off the deep end!

Pb 0-06-074518-5

#5: Miss Small Is off the Wall!

Could Miss Small, the gym teacher, be A.J.'s craziest teacher yet?

www.harperchildrens.com
www.dangutman.com

HarperTrophy®
An Imprint of HarperCollinsPublishers